P9-EJT-748

WHAT MOMMIES DO BEST

BY Laura Numeroff

ILLUSTRATED BY Lynn Munsinger

THIS BOOK IS A GIFT
OF FRIENDS
OF THE ORINDA LIBRARY

WITHDRAWN

SIMON & SCHUSTER BOOKS FOR YOUNG READERS

Mommies can teach you
how to ride a bicycle,

make a snowman with you,

and bake a delicious
cake for your birthday.

Mommies can help you
make a garden grow,

give you a
piggyback ride,

and take care of you
when you're sick.

Mommies can watch
the sun set with you,

sew the loose button
on your teddy bear,

and hold you when
you're feeling sad.

Mommies can take you
trick-or-treating,

help you give the
dog a bath,

and play with you
in the park.

Mommies can read you
a bedtime story,

tuck you in,

and kiss you good-night.

But best of all,
mommies can give you
lots and lots of love!

But best of all,
daddies can give you
lots and lots of love!

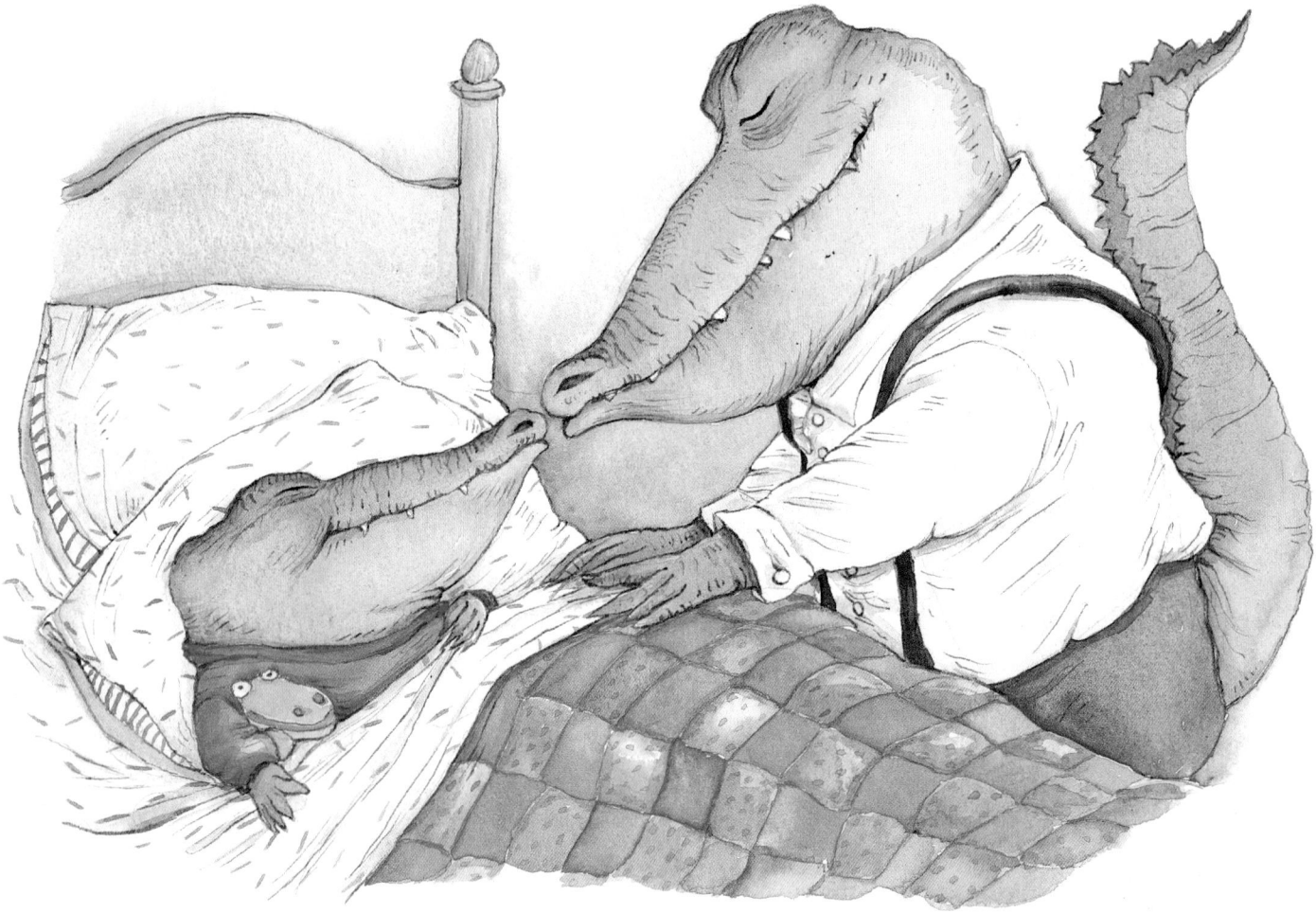

and kiss you good-night.

tuck you in,

Daddies can read you
a bedtime story,

and play with you
in the park.

help you give the
dog a bath,

Daddies can take you
trick-or-treating,

and hold you when
you're feeling sad.

sew the loose button
on your teddy bear,

Daddies can watch
the sun set with you,

and take care of you
when you're sick.

give you a
piggyback ride,

Daddies can help you
make a garden grow,

and bake a delicious
cake for your birthday.

make a snowman with you,

Daddies can teach you
how to ride a bicycle,

3190105148342O

WHAT DADDIES DO BEST